The FLORIDA Night Before Christmas

E.J. Sullivan

Illustrated by
Ernie Eldredge

SWEETWATER
PRESS

SWEETWATER
PRESS

The Florida Night Before Christmas
Copyright © 2005 by Cliff Road Books, Inc.
Produced by arrangement with Sweetwater Press

ISBN-13: 9781581733914
ISBN-10: 1-58173-391-7

Printed in China

The FLORIDA
Night Before
Christmas

ZZZZZZZZZ

'Twas a Florida night before Christmas,
and from the Panhandle to the Keys
Not a creature was stirring –
not a manatee sneezed.

Our stockings were hung
on the glass sliding doors,
Near Mom's sand-dollar wind chimes
from the new dollar store.

Baby Sister was lost in a sweet girlish dream
Of joining the Hurricanes cheerleading team.
And me in my Gator jammies, and Luke in his Seminoles tee,
Were watching the playoffs on our flat screen TV.

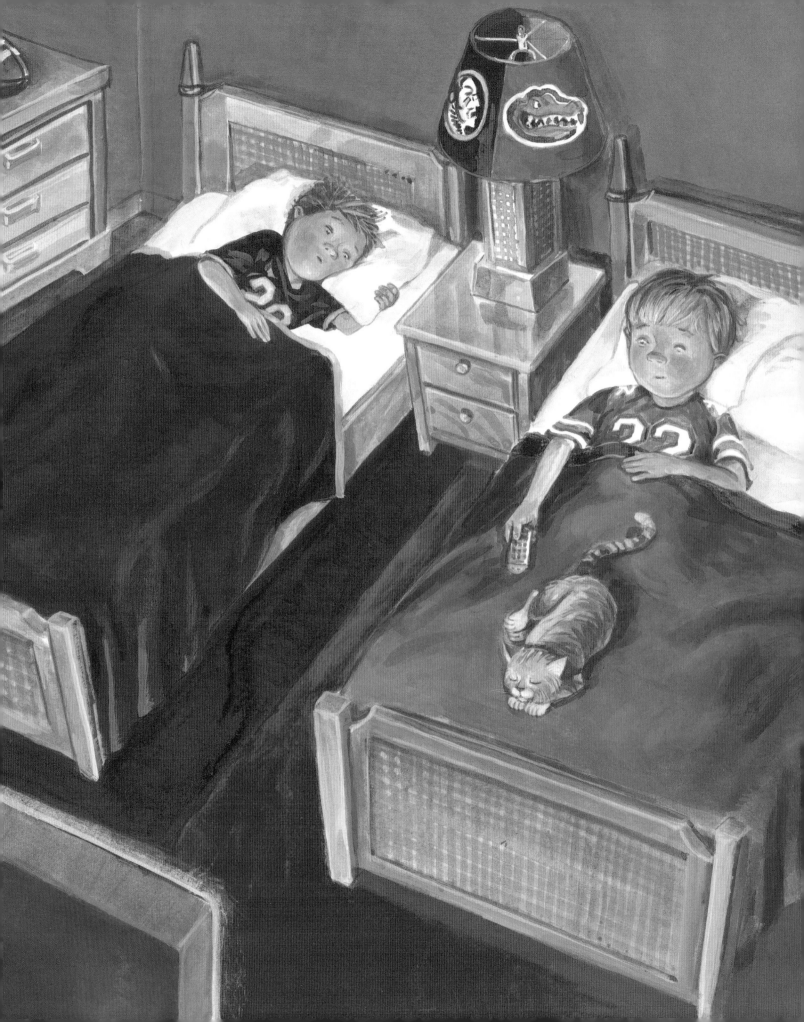

When out by the gas grill
I heard a noise like thunder –
It was louder than the start
of the Daytona 500!

I sprang to the window and
ran down the hall
Armed with Dad's bronze replica
Bowden football.

The moon was as bright as the malls in Orlando
Where Mom and Dad took us to look at a condo!
And then what to my wondering eyes should I spy
But an atomic-powered golf cart blazing on by!

With a little old driver
so lively 'n' quick,
He coulda rebuilt the Flora-Bama
ten times in a lick!

Eight semi-retired reindeer
    brought up the rear,
And he hollered so loud
    I could hear him from here:

"Hang on Milton, Shirley, Miguel, and Marie!
Hold on Herbie, Estelle, Jeb, and Cherie!
From the shores of Pensacola
    to the streets of St. Augustine —
Now fly to Miami, through Clearwater
    and Tarpon Springs!"

You know when we have to batten down the hatches
'Cause it looks like hurricanes are coming
　　　onshore in batches?
Well that's how this golf cart fired into action —
Kinda like Mom and Dad firing up
　　　over the presidential election!

About then I saw our big palm tree shake
When the bottom of that golf cart started to scrape.
I looked up through the branches and caught him red-handed —
On our Silver Springs birdhouse Santa'd crash landed!

Bless his heart. He was grinning like Buffett might be,
If he got himself tangled in the top of a tree.
Mom's always saying I should help folks who are older
So I helped him get down onto our John Deere mower.

Santa headed inside, slick
   as oysters in your pocket,
And filled all our stockings with boiled peanuts
   and bottle rockets.

Then he looked right at me,
    and before goin' out the door
Slapped on top of the TV
    some new bass fishing lures.

He fired up his golf cart
and soon they were gone,
All the while telling those deer
to hang on.
But I heard him holler out
as his rig sped away,
"Merry Christmas, Florida!
I wish I could stay!"